HOLIDAY MIRACLES

HOLIDAY MIRACLES

A CHRISTMAS/HANUKKAH STORY

ELLYN BACHE

 BANKS CHANNEL BOOKS

Published by Banks Channel Books
P.O. Box 80058
Simpsonville, SC 29680

Printed in the United States of America

ISBN: 1-889199-09-5
Library of Congress Catalog Card Number: 2001087899

Interior Illustrations: Angela Donato
Book Design: Carol Tornatore

Acknowledgments

The author would like to thank her husband, Terry Bache, for the 32 years of love and support that made this book possible.

She would also like to thank the members of her writers' groups for their continuing help and encouragement: Alyce Atkinson, Sharon Brown, Joyce Cooper, Beth Perry, Brooks Preik, Patricia Ruark, Nancy Tilly and Blonnie Wyche.

*In loving memory
of my mother-in-law,
Marian Bache*

1

"It's difficult to plan a Hanukkah party with a Christmas tree going up," Claire called teasingly across the hallway to her husband. "If not impossible."

"Then come help us," said Paul.

"Maybe later."

Sitting at the dining room table, Claire jotted the number twenty-five on a piece of paper, followed by a question mark. Twenty-five pounds of potatoes to feed sixty-five kids? Temple Shalom's preschoolers would eat two latkes at the most, and some wouldn't eat any. But the older children—ah! They were likely to inhale whatever Claire served them, in whatever quantity. Latkes, sour cream, apple sauce. Not to mention what the teachers would eat, or the women on the committee.

In the living room, Paul was perched on their none-too-safe step ladder, attaching strings of lights to the upper reaches of the tree. Normally they wouldn't need anything to climb on, but this year's tree was enormous—ridiculous, really—their biggest ever. Already the greenery was in place along the mantel, and a glossy foil streamer reading, "Happy Hanukkah!" strung along one wall. Though it was only the first of December, the annual neighborhood party was tomorrow, and people would be dropping by for *hors d'oeuvres*.

Still new to Christmas after fourteen years, Claire felt keyed up as she watched, expectant, even though the trees had turned out to be more troublesome than she'd imagined. So much work, such mess! One year their tree had begun shedding needles the minute they set it up. And the silver icicles, which Paul loved, always attached themselves to anything that passed within three feet of them, then dropped off all over the house. Claire's Jewishness left her no clout with which to veto the silvery threads—and the truth was, she wouldn't have outlawed them if she could. What would the holidays be like without icicles? The trimmings made her family so happy.

Right now her ten-year-old daughter, Sarah, was tenderly lifting each ornament from the storage box and removing its protective tissue paper, her chubby fingers working with surprising grace. She held each item up to the light for inspection, then placed it at the end of a neat line she was making on the sofa. Looking up, she spotted Claire in the dining room. Her eyes lit up, and she snapped her fingers. "Oh, I forgot!" she exclaimed, bounding up the stairs to her bedroom, returning seconds later at breakneck speed. Clutched in her fist was her newly-completed Sunday school project, a handmade clay menorah, painted what was supposed to be turquoise but had turned out an anemic blue. Proudly, Sarah nestled it among the branches on the mantel. "Hanukkah decorations!" she said.

Feeling herself flush with the excitement her daughter was radiating, Claire gave her a thumbs-up sign. "Good job!" She watched Sarah turn back to the storage box and carefully lift out a blown-glass rocking horse bought last year at an after-Christmas sale. "It's too good a deal to pass up," Sarah had insisted then, tugging furiously at Claire's coat. "Please, Mom. Look! Fifty percent off!" Claire had laughed at her daughter's shopping savvy and made the purchase. Now Sarah seemed as delighted to see the trinket as if she had discovered a long-lost friend. She patted the tiny horse's head and set it beside the other ornaments on the sofa.

In fact, Sarah seemed to be making the most of every moment, thrilled to be re-discovering the Christmas decorations without the help of her five-year-old brother, Louie. As wild as his sister was methodical, Louie usually thrashed through the wrappings, threw ornaments haphazardly out of the box, broke at least half a dozen, and generally drove his sister crazy. But this afternoon Louie was asleep—odd enough any time, but especially right now, close to the holidays.

Realizing that so much peace and quiet couldn't possibly be normal, Claire left her list on the table and headed into the den to check on her son. Louie escaped serious trouble most of the time because he was so affectionate and cheerful. But today his good disposition had deserted him. This morning he'd gotten up late, grouched around in front of the Saturday morning cartoons, and later grumbled his way through their trip to the cut-your-own Christmas tree farm. Part of the reason they'd selected this insanely huge tree was to cheer him up. It hadn't worked. When they stopped for lunch, he complained that his hamburger was cold. He poured mounds of ketchup on his French fries and then refused to taste them. The moment they got home he flung himself onto the couch and fell into this dead sleep. Claire attributed his strange behavior to the antibiotic he'd been taking for his latest strep throat. Under her gaze he opened one green eye, seemed to think better of it, and closed it again.

"Louie?" Normally he was up in an instant, with a mischievous a grin lighting his face. His current expression was closer to a scowl.

"Come on, boy. Time's a'wasting." Claire nudged him playfully. "Daddy's putting the lights on the tree. As soon as that's done you can start hanging the ornaments."

Louie grunted.

"Is that a yes? It sounds like a yes to me."

Reluctantly he stood up, groggily rubbed his stomach and scratched his back, and let Claire lead him into the living room.

Paul was still on the ladder, connecting a light to one of the upper branches. Although he hadn't set foot in a church since he graduated from high school, nevertheless Paul always treated their Christmas tree with a sort of religious fervor. It had to be a white pine, with long soft needles that wouldn't prick him as he worked. The lights had to be put in place first, onto the back branches where they would illuminate the other decorations from behind. Only then could the ornaments be hung: ornaments, Claire thought wistfully, which were once rather sophisticated and which now had acquired a dimestore quality reminiscent of the trees Paul's mother, Teresa, had when Claire first met her. Teresa decorated with every do-dad her six children ever made: colored tin-can tops, Styrofoam snowmen, cotton-ball wreaths. Teresa festooned her banister with plastic greenery, put plastic candles in every window in the house, set the table with plastic Mr.-and-Mrs.-Santa salt shakers that had been a gift from Joey, her youngest. Taking in the scene for the first time, Claire had decided how tasteful, how sophisticated, her own austere eye must be. But that was before she'd had children, who decorated equally inelegantly—and before she learned to love Teresa.

"There's my angel," Louie announced, seizing a white construction paper cut-out from Sarah's procession of ornaments on the sofa.

"Louie!" his sister scolded.

He paid no attention. The angel, which he'd made the year before in pre-school, had for its face a glued-on snapshot of Louie from the shoulders up, a surprisingly younger-looking, more babyish Louie. He studied it long enough to drive Sarah into a red-faced frenzy, then somehow set it back down without crushing it. Abruptly, he thrust a hand under his shirt and began scratching his stomach.

"What's the matter, honey?" Claire asked.

"I itch."

"Here, let me see."

Louie lifted his shirt. A round red welt adorned the ample belly he puffed out for everyone to see; another crimson splotch was rising at the bottom of his rib cage.

"He's getting a rash," Paul said.

"Oh, yuck," said Sarah.

"The antibiotic," Claire realized. "I'll bet he's allergic to the antibiotic."

"I thought he was almost finished with it."

"Well, he's certainly finished now," Claire said. "Does it itch everywhere? Or just in those two places?"

"Everywhere." Louie scratched his belly, then his back.

"I'll give you some medicine to make the itching stop."

Louie made a dramatic show of swallowing the liquid antihistamine Claire offered. After so many recent sore throats, he was used to downing spoonfuls of medicine and liked to make the most of the attention. Sarah turned away in disgust.

Claire wished she could dismiss Louie's condition so easily, but the idea of another allergic reaction in the family made her nervous. Several years ago, Sarah had climbed a tree into a nest of bees and received eleven stings. Her hands had puffed up despite doses of antihistamine, and six hours later she threw up. Reassurance from the doctor didn't temper Claire's inclination to rush her daughter to the emergency room until she realized that, once Sarah's stomach was empty, she was suddenly and thoroughly better. That one incident was all the experience with allergies Claire ever hoped to have.

"I'll call Dr. Roberts just to be sure," she said, aware that their pediatrician wouldn't be in the office on Saturday. As she expected, the answering service picked up and said he would call back. By the time the doctor got hold of her, Louie had developed a few more welts on his back and his stomach. He was hanging ornaments nonetheless—a little sluggishly

—and Dr. Roberts said she'd done the right thing: stopped the antibiotic, given him something for itching. "Generally these things work themselves out in twenty-four hours," he said. "He'll probably be better tomorrow."

"Time for the star!" Paul announced when she got off the phone. He brandished the large pointed ornament that went at the top of the tree—not shaped at all like a star and no longer the color of one, either, with its gold paint worn to a not-so-glossy tan. "Louie, you ready?" Paul asked.

"I'll do it!" cried Sarah, who knew perfectly well it was her brother's turn.

Claire braced herself for Louie's loud protest. But nothing came. He had flopped onto an overstuffed armchair, his eyelids half shut. In a moment he'd be napping again.

"Come on, you can climb the ladder," Paul cajoled, knowing how much his son loved heights, speed, danger.

"I don't feel like it."

"Let me!" Sarah shouted.

"Louie, are you sure?"

Nodding, Louie curled deeper into the chair and began to rub his belly.

"I think the antihistamine makes him sleepy," Claire said. "Louie, you can do the star next year instead. I'm sorry you don't feel well."

"I feel okay," said Louie, who had been known to proclaim himself healthy even during the acute stage of a stomach virus. Claire put her hand to his forehead and found it moist but not warm.

"Well, it's nice of you to let your sister have your turn."

Triumphant, Sarah ascended the ladder, with Paul behind her to hold her steady. "Good job!" Claire cheered. But she couldn't help her alarm at the angry red splotches popping up on her son's neck and arms.

The next morning, he was covered with them. Stomach, legs, even his earlobes.

"Scratch my back, Mommy," he murmured, so pathetically that Claire did.

She also dialed Dr. Roberts again,

who said this happened sometimes. "Continue the antihistamines and, if he itches a great deal, try giving him a bath. Water always soothes a rash."

"Could he be allergic to something besides the antibiotic?"

"It's possible, but I doubt it."

"Should we bring him in to see you? You said he'd be better today. I mean, how serious is this?"

"Probably not at all. But if there's a change, let me know." The doctor's voice seemed cool, metallic. Was he annoyed because she was calling on Sunday? He'd never seemed to resent his patients' intrusions, but until now they'd had so few emergencies that she really didn't know. Sarah's allergic reaction had happened—conveniently, Claire supposed—during the doctor's weekday office hours.

"Don't look so worried," Paul said when she hung up. "Take Sarah to Sunday School. Get out for a while, it'll do you good." He turned to Louie. "Come on, son, your old dad's going to give you a bath. Your dad's an expert at giving kids a bath." This was true enough. Paul had always bathed the children when they were little, taught them to blow soap bubbles through their fingers, helped them arrange their shampoo-laden hair into comical cones atop their heads. Louie, who had been lying silently on the bed, managed a slight, wan smile.

2

Temple Shalom was decorated for Hanukkah. Construction paper cutouts of Maccabee warriors adorned the bulletin boards, and elaborate drawings of menorahs sat on the desks in the classrooms. Downstairs, in the social hall, Sandy Cohen presided over the Judaica shop, selling a selection of Hanukkah items to raise money for the religious school.

Claire bought Louie a dreidle, a four-sided top with Hebrew letters on each side for playing the traditional Hanukkah game. You spun the top and, depending on what letter showed, won candy or pennies from the kitty, or had to put some in. A born gambler, Louie loved any game with an element of risk or luck, and this was one he could play even while he was sick. Claire used to forget which letters on the dreidle meant what. When she was a child, her family celebrated the holiday by lighting the candles in the menorah, feasting on roast chicken and latkes, and presenting Claire with a series of small gifts. But she didn't remember ever playing dreidle.

Ellyn Bache

For a few minutes, she sorted through the rolls of Hanukkah wrapping paper, blue and white backgrounds with cheerful, bright designs. She especially admired a pattern featuring shiny, golden Stars of David dancing across a textured field of white. "The wrapping paper gets prettier every year," she told Sandy Cohen.

Sandy, who selected all the items for the Judaica shop, beamed. "It is a nice selection, isn't it? How many rolls do you need?"

Embarrassed, Claire shook her head. Although she was completely out of paper, at the moment she didn't dare buy. An old superstition. She never planned for the future when the children were sick. If

36

she bought paper and wrapped gifts as if everything were going to be all right, something terrible might happen before Hanukkah actually arrived. In her skewed logic (and she knew it was skewed but couldn't do a thing about it), buying wrapping paper was entirely different from purchasing the dreidle. Louie could use the dreidle now, today. But Hanukkah was nearly two weeks away. No: she couldn't wrap Hanukkah gifts until Louie was better. Despite a college education, despite what she believed was her enlightened state of mind, when it came to the children she reverted to these pagan rites that had nothing to do with religion and everything to do with fear. She paid for the dreidle and rushed from the social hall, down the passageway to the temple's kitchen.

With a touch of a switch, the too-bright ceiling lights flicked on, and Claire sniffed the hint of gas that always wafted up from the pilot light on the old stove. Every year there was talk of renovating the kitchen. Claire had even volunteered for the committee to look into it, but so far nothing had been done. In the meantime she wanted to see what equipment was available for the latke party. Above the stove hung two enormous cast-iron pans, pitted with age but good enough for frying some of the latkes. The women on Claire's committee would also bring electric frying pans from home, and several food

Lakes (serves 4)
oil for frying
6 medium potatoes
1 small onion
2 eggs, slightly beaten
3 tablespoons flour
+ peper 1tsp salt
+ baking soda

processors for grating the potatoes and onions.

Mentally, Claire checked her list of supplies. Thirty pounds of potatoes (better to have too much than too little), flour, onions, pepper, salt. At least two gallons of oil. When she was a child, her mother tended to put her latkes in the pan before the oil got hot enough, with the result that they always came out greasy. Every year after they tasted them her mother laughed and insisted she'd do better on her next try—but by the time another Hanukkah rolled around, she always forgot. It hardly mattered, since they all enjoyed the latkes anyway. Claire always slathered hers with apple sauce while her father topped his with huge dollops of sour cream, and her mother, tactful, sampled a little of each.

Then all that changed. Claire's father died suddenly when she was ten, the same age Sarah was now. A few months later Claire moved with her mother to a smaller house in a nearby town, where somehow she was never enrolled in religious school or taken to services except on the High Holidays. Looking back, Claire thought her mother felt awkward going to temple without her father (something Claire sympathized with now) and found it easier not to join than to face a whole new congregation with only a half-grown daughter for company. Claire's most vivid "religious" memories from those years were of three weeks at a Jewish summer camp, where everyone wore freshly-laundered white shirts and shorts to Friday night services.

She didn't really go to temple again until she was an adult with children of her own. Sarah had just turned five, the right age for beginning some kind of Sunday School. Teresa offered to take her grand-daughter to the Catholic Church—would have been honored to, Claire knew. But Claire felt herself hesitating. She believed the children's religious training should be supervised by a parent, and talked it over with Paul.

It was a more difficult conversation than either of them expected. They'd had this talk years before and had never imagined repeating it would be necessary.

Of course they'd discussed the children's upbringing! They'd discussed it at great length when they decided to get married. But if they'd made any firm decisions then about religious training for children that might come along, neither of them could quite remember. Until Sarah and Louie were actually on the scene, it hadn't much mattered.

Now there seemed so much at stake that neither of them wanted to tackle it. Why cause trouble where there'd been none before? They went around and around, each trying not to say anything that would upset the other.

"It isn't that I'm not religious," Paul managed finally. "In many ways I think I am. But as to *organized* religion, I gave

43

it up a long time ago. So if you're asking if I could take Sarah to church—" He cleared his throat as if trying to dislodge some complicated emotion that was stuck there. "I don't want to raise a child who knows her father's a hypocrite."

"Paul, you're not—"

"I know I'm not a hypocrite—yet," he said. "And I don't want to be. Whatever you do, I'll support you. But I doubt I'll be much help." Then his voice grew gentle, dropped almost to a whisper. "It's up to you, Claire. Whatever you decide."

She mulled it over for weeks. She didn't want to hurt Teresa, but she couldn't task her mother-in-law with the responsibility of bringing up Sarah in the Church. Nor would she feel comfortable taking Sarah there herself, any more than Paul would. Her parents had raised her Jewish—she *was* Jewish, she realized, despite her half-hearted education. So finally she joined Temple Shalom. It still gave her a twinge to think how hurt Teresa must have been to know Sarah wouldn't be Catholic, though Teresa had never mentioned her disappointment and never would. And sometimes it saddened Claire to have to come here without Paul. But after five years at Temple Shalom, she felt comfortable. Louie had gone to the pre-school last year and started regular Sunday School just this fall. Two of Sarah's best friends were in her classes. For Claire and her children, Temple Shalom felt like home.

After she rummaged through the kitchen cabinets to make her inventory, Claire jotted down the missing items she'd need to buy for the party. The paper plates from the temple's supply were fine, but decorative Hanukkah napkins and cups would be much more festive. Debbie Eisenberg was making homemade apple sauce, but Claire would bring the sour cream. Then there was the orange drink and the— She lost her train of thought. Her mind rushed suddenly to Louie at home. Was he all right? Did the bath help? She feared, just for a moment, that perhaps even buying the dreidle was a risk.

3

By the time Claire and Sarah arrived home at noon, Louie was running a slight fever and picking at the welts on his arm.

"The water made him more comfortable for a while," Paul said, "but I don't think it had any long-term effect." Under Louie's fresh pajamas, the rash had deepened and spread. Examining her son's blotched belly, Claire felt the toast she had for breakfast clot and sit in a lump somewhere between her stomach and her throat. The only other time she had felt this way was the year her mother died.

Get hold of yourself, she silently admonished. Her mother's long illness had nothing to do with this. Even if Louie's rash wasn't from an allergy, the worst it could be was—what? Chicken pox? Louie had already had it. Measles? Nobody got measles anymore. Both children had had all their immunization shots. No reason to be such a bundle of nerves.

"What about the party?" she asked Paul, forcing herself to be practical. "The Wilsons"—their neighbors across the street—"could probably serve the *hors d'oeuvres* if we have to cancel."

"Oh, I think we'll be all right." Paul's voice was too hearty as he tried not to alarm Louie with the idea of canceling because he was sick. To Louie he said, "What if we call grandma and she comes and sits with you upstairs while the people are here?"

"What a good idea!" Claire agreed. But she was upset at how frightened Paul must be, not to want their son to be alone even for a moment while they entertained.

Teresa said of course she would come. She never refused when one of the children needed her, or one of the grandchildren. Sometimes Claire felt sorry for her mother-in-law, for having raised such a large family and for having,

49

really, so little else. But she knew it was silly to feel pity for someone who was always so content with her life—not just her family, but also her church and clubs and ever so many friends. Teresa was always cheerful, always willing to help. For all Claire knew, her mother-in-law might be canceling an outing with friends in order to pitch in during the party. This was something Teresa often did but never admitted—and right now, even if that was the case, Claire was enormously grateful. The company would start arriving at four. Several neighborhood women would bring *hors d'oeuvres* to add to those Claire had already tucked into the refrigerator for later. She and Paul would serve appetizers and drinks, and at six o'clock everyone would go to the Ebersole's for a light buffet before moving on to the Kinsley's for dessert. The progressive dinner had been a neighborhood tradition for as long as Claire could remember.

Having almost no work to do until right before the party, Claire turned to Louie, who was spinning his new dreidle without much enthusiasm. "Do you want to play the dreidle game?" she asked. "I have some time."

"Maybe later," Louie replied.

"Then how about a story? I can tell you about the Maccabees."

"We had that in Sunday School."

"Then you tell *me*." Louie loved to tell stories and maybe this would cheer him up. Hearing him would certainly cheer *her*. But he shook his head.

"No, you tell it," he said.

Claire did. "A long time ago a king named Antiochus ruled the Jewish people. A very evil king," she began. "Do you remember that part?"

Listlessly, Louie nodded.

"Instead of letting the Jews worship in their Temple in Jerusalem like they always did, he made a law that they had to worship idols or die. He sent his soldiers into the Temple to smash it up and burn the holy books and take the treasures," Claire said.

"And spill the oil," Louie murmured as if by rote.

"Yes. The Jews had a special lamp in

their Temple that was never supposed to go out. And the soldiers spilled the oil that was burned in the lamp. And then the Temple was dark. Do you know what happened then?"

"The soldiers put up idols, and let pigs run around." Louie's voice was flat.

"See? You know more than I thought you did!"

"Yes, but you tell it." He curled himself against her arm.

"Well, the Jews were very upset, but many of them were so frightened that they followed the new laws and bowed down to the idols. But a man named Mattathias wouldn't. He was angry. He decided to fight to get the Temple back. He took his five sons and hid out in caves in the mountains so the soldiers couldn't find them. Soon other Jewish warriors joined them, and they fought Antiochus's troops with whatever weapons they could find."

At the mention of weapons, Louie perked up. He made a gun out of his thumb and index finger and pointed it around the room.

"Oh, no, that was before guns were invented," Claire said. "I think they used things like spears and swords."

"Really?" Another blink of interest. Claire was so grateful that she rushed on, her voice breathless.

"Yes. And while the fighting went on, Mattathias got sick. He was an old man. But before he died he made his son,

Judah Maccabee, the new leader. Do you know what Maccabee means?"

"Hammer," Louie said, a little color in his cheeks.

"Right. The warriors were known as the Maccabees, the hammers. After a while they got so strong that Antiochus had to put together a huge army to send against them. But the Maccabees didn't give up. They kept hammering away. And finally they won! They drove Antiochus's troops out of the Temple. It belonged to the Jews again."

"But it was a mess."

"It sure was. The Jews were so happy to have their Temple back! And then they saw how it had been ruined. It was dark and dirty, and things were burned or broken up. But the Jews set out to clean the Temple and make it beautiful again."

"And to light the flame," Louie reminded her.

"Yes. But when they went to light the eternal flame that is never supposed to go out, they discovered that most of the special oil had been spilled or ruined. There was only enough to keep the light burning one day. They knew it would take at least a week to get more oil. But they lit the flame anyway."

"And when the oil was brought eight days later, the light was still burning!" Louie concluded with a reassuring burst of energy.

"That's why it's called the miracle of lights," Claire said. "That's why we have eight candles in the main part of the menorah and why we fry latkes in oil."

"And doughnuts," added Louie, who remembered this treat from past years. He furrowed his brow. "Will we get presents?"

"One present, on the first night."

"Michael Friedman gets a present all eight nights."

"That's because his parents are both Jewish," Claire told him. "He doesn't get to have Santa Claus."

"Oh. Right." Louie seemed unfazed.

Claire couldn't help feeling a bit smug. Her friend, Amanda, also in a mixed marriage, gave an elaborate Hanukkah party each year because she feared that otherwise her children, caught between religions, would be totally confused. Amanda tried to give Hanukkah the same weight and glitz as Christmas, while Claire insisted this wasn't only silly, it was impossible! Hanukkah was a minor Jewish holiday, one of many. How could it compete with a major Christian cele-bration? Why should it have to? And even apart from religious significance, how could it compete with TV Christmas specials and carols on the radio, with commercials for electronics and toys, with colorful displays in all the stores? It couldn't! No, Claire argued, the only way to cope was to let the children learn what Hanukkah was, and what Christmas was, and be trusted to understand the meaning of each.

And Claire believed they did. Despite Louie's certainty that his favorite holiday song was entitled, "Dreidle Bells," with a refrain of "Dreidle all the way," he didn't seem confused in any important way. It seemed perfectly normal to him that his friend celebrated only Hanukkah while he got to have Christmas, too. He and Sarah glided easily between Passover and Easter, Hanukkah and Christmas, drawing sweetness from both. Having listened to Claire's explanation about the presents, Louie was so far from being bewildered that he had fallen suddenly and peacefully asleep. Claire covered him with an afghan, kissed his blotchy face. Maybe it was only the parents who were confused.

In the living room Paul had turned

on the Christmas tree lights. He had even vacuumed. For the moment, the icicles were actually on the tree and not the rug. With the gold and blue and red lights reflecting off the ornaments and the tinsel, the room looked—in spite of the tree's outlandish size and amateur decorations—just as Claire believed it *should* look at Christmas. But the Maccabees were also on her mind, and she remembered that at Hanukkah her mother would get out the menorah, clean it until it shone, and let Claire help her light the candles each night. In her long eye of memory the holiday glowed: candles in the menorah, even greasy potato latkes fried in lukewarm oil. Funny. She wondered what her mother would think if she could see the scene before her now—mostly Christmas, a little Hanukkah. Would she disapprove? She wondered how, years from now, Louie and Sarah would remember the holidays. Would the confusion set in then? Once more she checked on Louie. His breathing was even, but his welts were such an angry red that she reminded herself she mustn't think of the future at all. Fighting the nausea that had welled up in her stomach again, she got her menorah down from the shelf in the china closet where it sat all year, and shined and shined and shined.

4

"You've heard the story about how Mark passed out after his cholera shot when he was in the Marines," Teresa said to Claire after the cocktail party. Mark was Paul's older brother. "But they can do so many things with allergies these days. Take care of it like it's nothing."

Claire was dialing Dr. Roberts again

as they talked. Louie's fever had shot up and now, despite a bath, it stood at 103. Claire and Paul had stayed behind while the guests moved on to the buffet.

"Oh, Teresa, I hope you're right," Claire said. She had always called Teresa by her first name though once, in the early years, Teresa indicated she would have preferred otherwise. And now, as Claire smiled at her mother-in-law to thank her for offering comfort, she felt a pang of guilt. Teresa looked very beautiful in the glow of the Christmas lights, a pale Irish beauty even at sixty-three, with hardly any wrinkles around the liquid green eyes which Paul and Sarah and Louie had all inherited. Yet there was something about Teresa's drawn expression that told Claire her mother-in-law was more concerned about Louie than she was letting on. When Dr. Roberts got on the line, Claire was sure she heard Teresa breathe an audible sigh.

"If it will make you feel any better, by all means bring him in," the doctor said. "I'm in my office anyway."

Claire gathered from this that he was humoring her, letting her bring Louie in on Sunday night because it happened to be convenient, but she was too worried to argue. They put Louie's coat over his pajamas, because the pajama fabric was softer against the welts than a shirt, and Paul carried him to the car. They didn't even put on his shoes.

Dr. Roberts was less condescending

in person than he'd been on the phone. He took one look at Louie and dropped his folly-of-overprotective-mothers attitude at once. "I'm glad you came in," he said as he probed Louie's belly and examined the welts.

"You do get reactions like this sometimes from this antibiotic," he said. "Not many reactions overall, but when they do occur, sometimes they're pretty wicked. The good news is, usually they're self-limiting."

He gave Louie an adrenaline shot and handed Claire some medicine samples.

"Bronchial dilators?" she read off the label.

"Breathing medicine. Just in case fluid builds up in his lungs. You probably won't need it."

Briefly, Claire was visited by the litany of soothing platitudes offered when her mother was sick. "One of those pesky chronic infections . . . probably nothing serious." Her mother was in and out of hospitals for months before a clear diagnosis was made, and by then she was too sick for the treatments to do any good. Why did Claire keep thinking of that? She'd taken both children to Dr. Roberts for years and had no reason to distrust him. Pushing her mind beyond her fear, she called up the doctor's words—"pretty wicked, but self-limiting." She could live with that. When they got home, Louie went to bed without complaint and slept all night.

By the next morning the welts had become nothing more than pale splotches, pallid memories of the night before. A little fever lingered, nothing to worry about. *Relax,* Claire told herself. Louie had had one infection after another all autumn. No wonder he was listless.

He lay on the couch in the den, watching the morning cartoons without much interest. Today he'd rest and gain strength; it was amazing how quickly children could recover. Tomorrow he'd be well enough to go to the grocery with her, buy potatoes and oil for the latkes, drop the supplies off at the temple. With luck he'd be back in school by Wednesday. She wanted this so much. Wanted to buy her Hanukkah wrapping paper, be normal again. Wanted to feel they had . . . escaped.

But she was uneasy. When Louie fell asleep in front of the TV, Claire dialed Teresa's number to thank her for sitting yesterday, perhaps to draw comfort from her mother-in-law's voice. The phone rang and rang. Teresa was the only person Claire knew who refused to turn on her answering machine unless she was out of town. Right now, she was probably at St. Ann's, where she went to Mass several mornings a week. Claire could picture her

there, kneeling in her pew, praying for Louie's health. The image made her smile.

For a moment, she was transported back to the first time she'd ever seen her mother-in-law praying, in the church where Paul's sister Lisa had gotten married. Teresa had been kneeling while the rest of the worshippers stood, clasping her hands in front of her, completely at ease. Claire, who had been in a Catholic Church only two or three times and who felt strange and ill-at-ease in that unaccustomed, cathedral-like place, had been unexpectedly glad to see Teresa so engrossed. She herself could not have prayed under those daunting stone arches even for Lisa's happiness, and she liked Lisa very much. After growing up as an only child, it meant a lot to Claire to be part of Paul's big family. She wanted Lisa not only for a sister-in-law but for a friend. She had felt, somehow, that her mother-in-law was praying for all those things on her behalf.

Now she drew hope from the idea of Teresa praying at St. Ann's for Louie. If Claire prayed in temple and Teresa prayed in church, perhaps they would have a double line, as it were, to God. Perhaps He would hear one of them. She knew this was probably as illogical as her superstition about making plans when the children were sick, but there it was. Paul's sister Lisa was a close friend with a happy marriage—because of Teresa's prayers? And Louie would get well. A silly notion, maybe even childish—but it made her feel much better.

5

That evening, Louie dozed on Claire's bed as she phoned her latke party committee. The event would be held toward the end of Hanukkah, and the eight-day holiday hadn't even started yet, but Claire wanted to set up a schedule well in advance. She'd call the whole committee again later to go over the details. Better too many reminders than too few.

"We'll need at least an hour to peel all the potatoes and chop them before we start cooking," she told Susan Friedman.

"And to set the tables," Susan added. "Maybe we should allow an hour and a half."

Claire was considering this when Louie started coughing. She didn't pay much attention at first, because children often coughed in their sleep. Then she realized it was not an ordinary cough at all but a deep rasp—*huh, huh, huh*—a rolling and rumbling of phlegm, over and over without resolution. As if he were choking on his own lungs.

"I'll call you later." She hung up and tried to nudge Louie awake. "Honey, sit up." But Louie slept on, coughing convulsively. For the briefest instant Claire caught a glimpse of the two of them in the mirror across the room: mother and child in the glow of golden lamplight, in bedspread-tones of red and gold; the boy uneasy in his own chest, the woman paralyzed, thinking, perhaps he is not sleeping at all but unconscious, suffering, while she was chatting on the phone. "Paul!" she screamed.

Paul rushed up from downstairs, where he and Sarah had been sitting by the tree, listening to their favorite Christmas music. When Paul entered the room and saw Louie, his rosy complexion turned to ash.

"Hey, Louie, wake up, son," he said, lifting the boy in his arms. "Wake *up*."

Finally—disoriented, irritable—Louie did.

They gave him the breathing medicine, unopened until now, and rushed him to the car. In the emergency room minutes later, Louie's breathing was less labored, but he was admitted to the hospital for tests and observation.

The next twenty-four hours were a nightmare. Wired into IV tubes and monitors, Louie was examined, poked, prodded. At first he cried and vented his anger, but then, seeing that Claire and Paul weren't going to stop the torture, he divorced himself from it all and submitted to his treatment as if he were somehow absent. Not part of it. Not there.

Even when Teresa came, bearing a

gift of one of the hard-to-get racing cars in a set Louie had been collecting, he only nodded dully and closed his eyes, pretending to be asleep.

"Well, I don't blame you," Teresa whispered as she bent to kiss him. "You'll feel a whole lot better when you get out of here. Which won't be long at all."

To Claire, in the corridor outside Louie's room, Teresa said, "I meant that. He'll be fine once they spring him. Imagine being his age and faced with—this." She indicated the brightly painted but antiseptic-smelling hall of the children's wing. Claire didn't mention how clearly this brought back the odor of the hospital where her mother once lay.

"Paul was just five when he had his

tonsils out, and until we took him home he was as withdrawn as Louie is," Teresa went on. "But he survived it, and so will Louie." Teresa touched a gentle finger to Claire's cheek. "And so will you."

Louie was released from the hospital the next morning, but his strange mood persisted. Even after several days passed and his fever subsided, Claire would have been hard-pressed to call him recovered. He napped, ignored his toys, stared into space.

"Probably a little depression," Dr. Roberts said. "Not unusual. Let him resume a few of his activities."

Claire invented an errand. "Come

on, Louie, I have to drop some groceries at the temple," she said. "It'll make you feel better to get out. Afterwards we can get a hamburger at McDonald's."

"I'm not hungry."

"Oh, you'll be surprised." She dressed him for the first time all week. At the temple Claire was slow going down the stairs because she was loaded down with groceries. But instead of racing ahead of her like he usually did, Louie acted as if it was all he could do to keep up.

"Are you okay?" she asked as she set her bags on the counter in the kitchen.

"My shoes are too tight," Louie announced.

"What do you mean, your shoes are

81

too tight? They're practically new."

"Well, they hurt." With theatrical flair, Louie slumped to the floor and refused to budge.

Claire recognized her son's familiar dramatics, but she was too cautious to ignore him. "All right, let me see."

Sure enough, when she took his shoe off, ugly red lines marked where the tongue had pressed in, and his whole foot was puffy. Claire's throat closed like a vise. After all those tests in the hospital, *this*?

"It isn't unusual," Dr. Roberts reassured her when she arrived unannounced at his office. "With a reaction like this, it takes time for the swelling to go down." But the warning he issued was bleak: "If anyone ever gave him this antibiotic again, it could be life-threatening."

Claire thought of her mother's illness, and her stomach contracted like a muscle.

6

On the Friday night before the start of Hanukkah, Claire went to temple with Sarah, whose Sunday School class was helping with the Friday night service. Each student was to read a portion from the prayer book, including a few lines in Hebrew. Claire remembered only a few of the Hebrew letters and couldn't read the

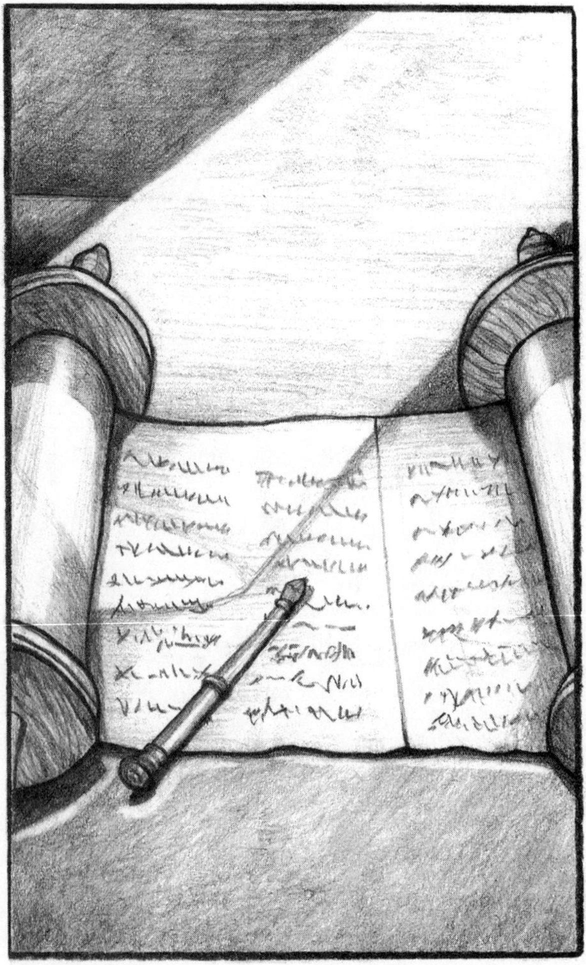

text at all anymore, but most of the service was in English, and she knew some of the prayers by heart. As the choir sang and the organ played and the congregation read, she found the words soothing, familiar.

You shall love the Lord your God with all your mind, with all your strength, with all your being.

She remembered reading this passage as a child, sitting between her parents, breathing her mother's perfume.

Set these words, which I command you this day, upon your heart. Teach them faithfully to your children; speak of them in your home and on your way, when you lie down and when you rise up.

The words were very beautiful to her: a chant, a hosanna.

Bind them as a sign upon your hand; let them be a symbol before your eyes.

But wait—she had done none of this. The thought of her laxness began to draw off the beauty of the words. Perhaps this was her failing: to have married Paul, to have dangled her children between two religions, to have offered no clarity of thought.

Inscribe them on the doorposts of your house, and on your gates.

Take the clear path. Perhaps Louie's illness was her punishment for not doing that.

This sounded crazy.

Or was it?

The rabbi's sermon, as always at this time of year, was about the dangers of assimilation. Christmas is seductive, he said. Sometimes Jews get so wrapped up in the tinsel that they forget who they are. Claire had always found this particular sermon difficult to take. Being married to Paul, she had obviously assimilated more than the rabbi would have liked, and he seemed to be accusing her of something. In the past, she'd tried hard to shrug off her irritation. She had always believed, secretly, that God required something different from each person. From Teresa, her Catholic devotions. From Paul, his steadiness, perhaps even his conviction that religion had less to do with churches and synagogues than with moral principles and faith. She had always imagined that God enjoyed being worshipped in different ways—that He delighted in the incense of the Catholic High Mass, the solemn simplicity of the Quakers, the joyous singing at the A.M.E. Zion Church.

But tonight she wasn't so sure. Her religious theories were no more sophisticated than they were when she was five, full of independent musings and superstitions. Perhaps God required, from Claire at least, a little more straightforward Jewishness.

Having come down from the *bimah* after her class finished reading, Sarah sat through only half the sermon before she began to fidget. Claire shot her a warning glance, which quieted her for a moment. But soon she began turning around to signal her friend Becky in the row behind them, and moments later the two little girls were tittering behind fingers held up to their mouths. "Stop," Claire hissed. Services might seem long to a ten-year-old, but Sarah had to learn. Claire frowned, trying to look as fierce as possible. Then she remembered the conversation she and Teresa had had the last time they were out for their weekly Wednesday lunch, and she couldn't suppress a smile.

"The kids always make such a fuss in services that I don't ever know what to do," Claire had confessed to her mother-in-law. "Other kids seem like little angels and mine are-well, you know, so *bad*."

"Bad? I don't know about *that*," Teresa joked. "Sarah and Louie certainly seem like little angels to *me*."

"You should just see them. At the last children's service Louie sneaked in some bubble gum and popped a huge bubble as loud as he could and let it splatter all over his face."

"I bet the other children were delighted." Teresa grinned and took a sip of the white wine the two of them always had on Wednesdays, which made them feel daring and naughty.

"The children might have been delighted, but the mothers weren't," Claire said.

"Well, if it makes you feel any better,

my six weren't very quiet in church, either." She set her glass down on the table and leaned toward Claire conspiratorially. "You know, you can't actually say much when kids are acting up in church, but sometimes I would reach over and give them a little pinch," she whispered. "It's silent—and nobody sees it."

"I don't believe it!" Claire hooted. She couldn't imagine Teresa pinching.

But Teresa nodded emphatically. "Oh yes, I pinched them many times!"

At the very absurdity, the two of them giggled together like schoolgirls.

Now Claire wondered how her closeness to this woman could be wrong. Or her love for Paul, who was religious but not observant. Or her passing down

Paul's joyful ritual of the Christmas tree, along with Hebrew lessons and latkes and her own ancient faith. Could all this really be a terrible mistake?

After the service there was an *oneg shabbat,* a social hour with cakes and coffee prepared by the Sister-hood. Everyone asked about Louie. "Wonderful!" they exclaimed when they heard he was out of the hospital.

"Well, he's still not very chipper," Claire said.

"Oh, he'll be fine, you'll see. He needs a little time."

Claire hoped they were right, but even so, their offhandedness upset her. Louie had been lying on the couch all day with vacant eyes, not really even watching television. Was this the same child who a few weeks ago had tried to negotiate more TV time with a politician's slickness? "I'll clean my room," he'd promised, to which Claire had retorted, "Louie, you never clean your room. Never." He'd cocked his head in disbelief, as if Claire were too simple to understand. "How can you be sure I won't clean it this time?" he'd asked. "Unless we make a deal, how can you be *absolutely sure*?"

Then, when she'd still refused, Louie had good-naturedly abandoned his argument and gone out to ride his bike instead. Maybe that was worse. He wove so haphazardly down the middle of the street, his training wheels making his route so wobbly and unpredictable, that

Claire had to run after him and make him stop. Louie seemed genuinely puzzled when she scolded him about not watching for cars. "They won't hit me," he'd insisted, laughing at her concern, believing he was invincible.

Was this the same child who no longer cared about TV? Who didn't go outside because he seemed too frightened, too weak?

As the voices of Claire's friends swirled around her, the brownie in her mouth began to taste like ash. The knotting filled her stomach, the feeling she'd carried around the whole time her mother was dying. Why did she feel this way? What did it mean? As her friends and the doctor had all pointed out, Louie probably only needed a little time. But illness had never affected Louie's disposition before, even when he was a lot sicker than he was now, with stomach flu or a throat so sore he could hardly swallow.

All she knew was that she was frightened. All she knew was, she didn't understand it. Louie no longer smiled. Louie no longer fit into his shoes.

7

A few hours before the sunset that would mark the beginning of Hanukkah, Paul came home from work early to watch the children while Claire made a quick trip to the temple's Judaica shop to buy wrapping paper. She felt like a fool, procrastinating so long because of an old superstition. She had to close herself in her bedroom so the children wouldn't see her, sitting on the floor surrounded by scissors and tape and gifts. In any case, Louie wasn't any better just because she'd waited. Not better, not worse. They were living in limbo, day to day.

She was furiously cutting the paper, angry with herself, worried about Louie, feeling frustrated and helpless, when Paul knocked softly and let himself into the room.

"I was going to wait," he said, "but I thought I'd give this to you now." He held out a tiny box, wrapped in the signature white brocade paper of the town's best jeweler. The box was topped by a satiny blue bow.

"Oh, Paul, you shouldn't—" Claire

began, but he put a gentle finger to her lips. "Open it," he said.

Inside, on a field of deep blue satin, lay a gold pendant. Simple but beautifully crafted, it was shaped like a perfect, fluted milkshake glass with two straws. Claire took one look and burst into tears.

It reminded her of everything. And most especially, it reminded her that she'd been thinking and acting like a fool. What was wrong with her? After fourteen happy years, how could she have imagined even for a moment that marrying Paul was a mistake, in God's view or anyone else's? When you fell in love over something as sweet as a milkshake, it couldn't possibly be a blunder. It was a gift of fate.

She'd met Paul her second year out of college while working in a town hundreds of miles from here, at the diner where she usually stopped for a take-out lunch. The Milky Way, the place was called. It had been in business as long as anyone could remember, equally famous for its hamburgers and its homemade ice cream.

That day, as she'd waited for her order, she'd watched a young man take his tray and sit down alone at a nearby table. In front of him he placed two huge chocolate milkshakes. Most people couldn't even drink one.

Though usually a bit shy, Claire found herself staring as the man sipped the thick liquid through a straw and spooned up the solid ice cream from the bottom of the fluted glass. She liked the way he ate, gracefully but with gusto. She wondered why she hadn't noticed him before. The lunch crowd was pretty predictable, the same people almost every day. She was still staring when the man looked up, and Claire found herself gazing directly into the green depths of his dark-lashed eyes. Embarrassed, anxious to seem clever rather than vulnerable, she blurted out quickly, "You must be a mighty thirsty man."

Paul blushed. She couldn't remember seeing a man blush like that before. Then, instantly, he recovered. "Oh, no," he said easily. "The other milkshake is for you."

"I've heard lines before," she laughed, "but this one takes real nerve."

"All right," he conceded. "You don't necessarily have to drink it. But if you join me I'll tell you all about my thirst."

And somehow, instead of rushing back to the office with her hamburger and fries, she did. Although she expected some outrageous story, she was curious enough to want to hear it. It surprised her to realize he was probably telling the truth.

As a child, he had lived in this town with his family. "We were six brothers and sisters," he said, "and when we were particularly good—which wasn't that often—Mother would bring us here for a treat. She'd order three milkshakes,

104

and we'd each get half. It was wonderful, but it was never enough. I used to dream at night of drinking a whole Milky Way milkshake. It was my goal.

"Then we moved away, and I never got to do it. I always told myself if I ever came back here, I'd not only drink a whole milkshake, I'd drink two. I'd drink Milky Way shakes until they made me sick." A satisfying gurgle through the straw signaled that he'd reached the bottom of the first glass. He started on the second. "To tell you the truth, I think I'm about at that point now."

He made a terrible face, rolling his eyes and pretending to gag. It was at that moment, before she even knew his name, that Claire fell hopelessly in love.

Paul told her he was in town on business, just for a week. They went out every night and met at the diner every day for lunch. They ate Milky Way hamburgers and shared Milky Way milkshakes, bending their heads together as they sipped from a single glass through two straws. They sampled vanilla, strawberry, chocolate, and eggnog. They decided eggnog was an acquired taste.

Six months later, they were married.

"Hey," Paul said now as he wiped away the tears streaming down Claire's cheeks. "I thought this would cheer you up."

"Oh, it does," Claire said as she lifted the necklace from the box. "It truly does."

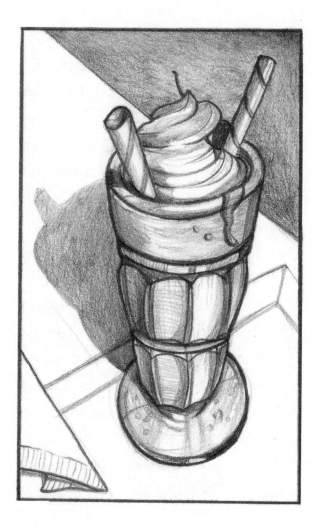

Her rejuvenated mood lasted the rest of the afternoon. When the sun went down, Claire and Sarah said the Hanukkah blessings together as they lit the *shammes*, the "helper" candle, and then used it to kindle the first of the eight candles in the main part of the menorah. Tomorrow they would light two candles, and one more each night after that.

Afterwards, Claire kissed her daughter on the cheek, proud of Sarah's good Hebrew, and how well she'd remembered the prayers. Paul seemed mildly amused by the whole procedure. Louie wanted to blow the candles out.

"You know better," Claire admonished jokingly. "You know we let them burn until they go out themselves. To remind us of the light in the Temple that burned for eight days even though there wasn't enough oil."

Louie only shrugged. The house was warm, and his complexion was splotchy. He always got splotchy when he was overheated lately, a frightening reminder of the welts that had gone away.

Claire had spent hours preparing the traditional holiday meal. Along with a homemade challah and vegetables and trimmings, she served a roast chicken Louie only picked at and golden latkes he didn't touch at all. For dessert, they had doughnuts, also fried in oil for the holiday, which Louie consented to eat.

Finally, Claire brought out the presents. Sarah, who had suddenly become a clothes buff, said she adored her new sweater. Louie, who had requested a certain miniature racing car for his collection, admired his gift politely but without excitement. And when Sarah suggested they play dreidle, he said no.

"I bet you don't even remember what the Hebrew letters stand for on the dreidle," Claire teased.

"They stand for 'A Great Miracle Happened There,'" he replied apathetially. "We learned that in Sunday School."

Feeling rebuffed, Claire touched her fingers to the milkshake pendant at her throat, hoping to recall some of her earlier joy. But it was too late. It didn't help.

In his sleep that night, Louie had one of his coughing spells. He hadn't slept through a single night without one. Claire gave him his medicine, which quickly calmed the spasm. But even after he fell asleep again, Claire was too restless to go back to bed. Why should Louie still be coughing? Was the medicine covering up something else that was wrong? Dr. Roberts didn't think so. But Claire wasn't sure. She stalked the house, touched the cold menorah, picked up the unused dreidle lying on the table beside it. A Great Miracle Happened There, she thought. But not here.

On Wednesday, Teresa appeared at noon, carrying a huge bag and a bottle of white wine. "We can't go out with Louie still at home," she said, lifting a platter of Greek salad from the bag with a flourish, "but we still have to eat."

In her shopping bag were also lovely paper plates from the Hallmark shop: expensive, festive plates with a neutral design that didn't suggest any particular holiday, and decorative plastic wine goblets—"so you won't have to wash."

"Oh, Teresa, you shouldn't have gone to so much trouble!" Claire exclaimed. But she found herself admiring the food. She hadn't felt this hungry for days.

While Teresa uncorked the wine and Claire set the table, Louie nibbled a peanut butter sandwich as if it were cardboard. The two women exchanged glances. By the time they were ready to eat, Louie had abandoned his food and fallen asleep. Claire remembered with real alarm how much she used to have to fight with him to take a nap.

Between Claire and Teresa at the table was Claire's menorah. They were already sitting down before Claire realized she'd forgotten to move it. Though Teresa would never complain, Claire sensed the sight of it hurt her—not so much because it represented Claire's Jewishness or even Paul's fallen-away Catholicism, as because it signified the things they couldn't share at a time like this, when they were both so worried about Louie

113

and would have found it comforting to be closer.

With astonishing clarity, Claire remembered the first visit she and Paul made to Teresa's after their honeymoon fourteen years ago, when she'd asked her new mother-in-law what she'd like to be called. "Well, *mother* would be nice," Teresa had said. But Claire, whose own mother had died less than a year before, couldn't do it.

Sensing the problem, Teresa had smiled gently. "Well, Teresa then," she'd said brightly. And so it had been, ever since.

Now Claire wished she'd responded differently. When it came to religion, Teresa believed, so strongly, what she believed. In some ways, so did Claire. When it came to religion, the two women would always follow different paths. But Claire might have called Teresa *mother* all those years ago; they might have shared that. It would have been another bond between them, something to hold onto no matter what. Now salads glistened on their plates, their cups of wine sparkled in the sunlight, and Louie dozed, pale and ill before them—-this child they both loved—and it seemed fourteen years too late.

8

At Louie's next checkup, Dr. Roberts took another throat culture. He didn't seem to know what else to do. This was how it had started, with a throat culture, when Louie first got sick. Before the antibiotic. Round and round they went, the circle going nowhere.

"He's still splotchy," Claire reported.

117

"Whenever he gets warm."

"Sometimes these skin reactions are very pervasive. He may always get splotchy when he gets warm. For the rest of his life."

The rest of his life.

"His shoes fit a little better, don't they?" the doctor asked hopefully.

"I don't know," Claire said. She had put him into a pair of Sarah's outgrown sneakers. He hadn't worn his own shoes for weeks.

Claire was getting Louie dressed and ready to leave when Dr. Roberts came back into the room. "This is a surprise," he said, holding up a printed report. "Louie's throat culture was positive for strep. I think this is what we've been missing." He arched an eyebrow and nodded with what looked like satisfaction. "The infection is still there and is feeding into the allergy. In effect, he's allergic to the strep."

To Claire this sounded ridiculous. So it was when her mother was sick: one explanation and then another, the diagnosis never really clear until it was too late. The knot in her stomach grew tighter. She couldn't remember when she didn't have the knot.

"I'm prescribing another antibiotic, chemically unrelated to the first one," the doctor said. "He shouldn't be allergic to it. It should take care of the infection."

"And if he doesn't get better?"

"There's no point thinking about

that. No reason why this shouldn't work. Look at him. He's already better than he was. Aren't you, buddy?"

"Sure," Louie agreed flatly.

Not much better, Claire thought. Not really.

Louie took the new medicine, but he didn't perk up. Mostly he sat in front of the TV, ignoring reruns of Christmas specials he usually adored. He didn't smile, didn't play. One day, when Claire caught a glimpse of him from across the room, a tremor of real fear caught at the back of her throat. There had been a moment, during her mother's illness, when a vacantness had come over her features and Claire knew she had given up. She saw that expression on Louie's face now.

No! she thought.

"Listen, Louie," she told him. "I know you still feel kind of ratty. But you can't let it get the best of you. Part of getting better is up to you." *Not always,* she thought. But she made herself continue. "You have to make up your mind."

"Right," Louie said without expression.

That night Paul came home from work and dropped a package from Wal-Mart on their bed. "Christmas wrapping paper," he explained. He'd been pretending he didn't know why

121

Claire had waited until the last minute to wrap her Hanukkah presents or why she hadn't bought Christmas paper yet, though the holiday was practically upon them. But he had made his point.

The next day, while Louie napped away the long, gray afternoon, Claire sneaked upstairs and wrapped a few Christmas gifts, even spent time cutting different colors of ribbon and tying fancy bows. There were too many packages to do all at once, and no matter what happened, someone was likely to want the gifts when the time came. They might even appreciate her efforts to make them look special. Hesitating any longer made no sense.

Where had her superstitions gotten

her, anyway? She'd been so careful to live day to day, not to make plans, and yet here they were, weeks later, with nothing really resolved. She was beginning to think there was enough real confusion, in this muddle of beliefs and holidays and feelings, without her fearful rituals. Perhaps what was important was doing what little tasks she could, even if that meant planning for Christmas morning while her menorah burned and her son lay ill. She had made her choices. She wouldn't change them even if she could. She wrapped her presents and tried to put her superstitions aside.

By the end of the week, Louie's skin seemed less splotchy, no matter how hot it got in the house. And one bitter cold night, he slept soundly until morning without coughing at all.

"Ten hours straight," Claire reported cautiously when Teresa called. "But that might not mean anything."

"Well, I prayed for him at Mass." Since the illness, Teresa had gone every morning.

"I should call you Mother Teresa after all this," Claire teased. "You deserve the Nobel Prize!"

Teresa chuckled. "I always thought Mother Teresa was a wonderful example. Even when I was a little girl, I thought it would be nice to be a nun."

"No!" Claire exclaimed.

"Oh, yes. I thought it would be a lovely life. But instead I had six kids, and I can't say I regret it."

"Well, maybe not Mother Teresa then. Maybe just *mother*." After so much turmoil, the words flowed as smoothly as Wednesday's wine.

There was a slight pause on the other end. Then Teresa said, a little breathlessly, "Well, that I *would* like."

9

Louie napped less in the daytime, slept more at night. The coughing disappeared. But he refused to dress, and he had grown so serious that Claire could hardly believe he was the same child who last summer hung upside down from a limb of their oak tree and called, "Mom, look!" just to elicit her expression of horror. How could

a few weeks' illness have transformed him
so? Made him so introspective and afraid?
And yet it had.

If there was any improvement, it was
only that Louie's interest had revived in
the Christmas specials, which were on
TV almost every day now. Rudolph the
Red-Nosed Reindeer. The Waltons. The
Grinch. He and Sarah were in the den
watching one of them as the last night
of Hanukkah approached, the evening of
the latke party. Claire only half listened
as she cleaned the food processor she'd
take to Temple Shalom for grating the
potatoes. Everything else was already
packed and ready.

"I'm leaving in exactly twenty minutes," she called to them. "Louie, if you

want to go, get ready. I can't be late." She knew she sounded harsh. She also knew Louie would opt to stay home with Paul. The cheerful, buoyant child she knew was gone.

She rinsed the processor and listened to snatches of *The Little Drummer Boy* from the other room. She used to like *The Little Drummer Boy* very much—or any stories of miracles, now that she thought of it. She always hoped some of them were true; she never cared which ones. The Jewish Maccabees, the Christian Nativity. *The Lord is One,* the prayer book said. Back then, she'd believed that any miracle would be proof.

She could see the television only dimly from the kitchen; the drummer boy playing for the baby Jesus, offering his meager gift. And now—oh yes, she remembered it very well—right now the drummer boy's little lamb was being healed; this always made her cry. The boy was holding his pet; his gift of love and music had been accepted; the lamb was suddenly well.

"Oh Mommy, do you see *that*?" Louie called from the den. Even in the flickering light, Claire saw color in Louie's face, noticed his smile. And something else: he was fully dressed for the latke party. In pants and shirt. And shoes.

"Louie?" She was incredulous.

"I made up my mind to get dressed."

He wore a plaid shirt and last year's

favorite checked pants, two inches too short. One of his socks was white, the other gray.

"Mommy?" Louie called.

Claire stared at him, stunned less by the outfit than the clarity of what she should have known all along. The miracles were all the same, always had been. One miracle, arching over human frailties and sorrows and differences like a rainbow. When she had lost her parents, it had given her another. And now here was her son, restored, exercising the fashion sense of a clown.

The miracle was love.

"Mommy, let's go!" Louie persisted. "Boy, you weren't kidding when you said old people move *slow*." He grinned, then cocked his head, studying her, growing serious. "Mommy? Are you okay?"

Claire nodded but didn't speak right away because she was standing at the sink with tears in her eyes, thinking, *I must tell mother, I must tell Paul.* In the midst of the confusion there was suddenly no confusion at all. Teresa would be Mother; Louie would do wheelies in the street. One day's oil would burn for eight days, and a Child would be born. And Claire would feel for a long time as she did right now—that quite unexpectedly, in spite of everything—she had been lifted into a state of grace.